SCOOBY-DOO!

THE CASE OF THE CHEESE THIEF

written by
J. E. Bright

illustrated by
Scott Neely

THE MYSTERY INC. GANG!

SCOOBY-DOO

SKILLS: Loyal; super snout
BIO: This happy-go-lucky hound avoids
scary situations at all costs, but he'll do
anything for a Scooby Snack!

SHAGGY ROGERS

SKILLS: Lucky; healthy appetite
BIO: This laid-back dude would rather
look for grub than search for clues,
but he usually finds both!

FRED JONES, JR

SKILLS: Athletic; charming
BIO: The leader and oldest member
of the gang. He's a good sport – and good
at them, too!

DAPHNE BLAKE

SKILLS: Brains; beauty
BIO: As a sixteen-year-old fashion queen,
Daphne solves her mysteries in style.

VELMA DINKLEY

SKILLS: Clever; highly intelligent
BIO: Although she's the youngest member
of Mystery Inc., Velma's an old pro at
catching crooks.

SCOOBY-DOO!

The secret recipe for a million-dollar mozzarella is stolen onboard a European train trip! Only YOU can help Scooby-Doo and the Mystery Inc. gang solve this case of the cheese burglar.

Follow the directions at the bottom of each page. The choices YOU make will change the outcome of the story. After you finish one path, go back and read the others for more Scooby-Doo adventures!

YOU CHOOSE the path to solve...

THE CASE OF THE CHEESE THIEF

"Rhat's rext?" Scooby-Doo asks.

"What did you say, Scooby? Rats?!" exclaims Daphne Blake.

"Nope," says Norville "Shaggy" Rogers. "Scoobs just wants to know, like, what's our next destination on this train trip."

Sitting on a bench across their snug sleeper compartment, Velma Dinkley adjusts her glasses. "Well, we left Rome a couple of hours ago," she answers. "Next is Florence, then Bologna–"

"Raloney?" asks Scooby hungrily.

"Bologna," replies Fred Jones. "It's an Italian city. Maybe they invented baloney?"

Turn the page.

"Baloney is based on mortadella sausage, which was first made in Bologna," explains Velma. "Anyway, after that we're riding through Venice and Milan, which are also in Italy. Then the train reaches the Alps, and we'll cross those mountains into Geneva in Switzerland. In France, we end up in Paris, where we fly back home."

"Italy is so pretty," Daphne says with a sigh, staring out the window at the lovely landscape. "It was nice of the Prime Minister to give us this trip across Europe as thanks for finding his missing parrot. And it's a vacation, too – no mysteries to solve!"

"Not yet, anyway," says Fred.

"Trouble seems to find us," adds Shaggy, shuddering.

"Rouble!" Scooby added.

"I know something we're ready to handle – dinner! Right, Scoobs?" Shaggy asks.

"Rum-rum!" Scooby-Doo shouts.

The gang walks single file down the corridor on one side of the train. They step carefully, getting used to the rolling movement of the train chugging along its track.

The decor is cosy and old fashioned, with navy carpets, wood panelling on the walls, and gold curtains on the windows.

Fred leads them along two more sleeper carriages. He pushes through heavy doors in the segments between carriages, which are enclosed by thick rubber accordions all around. They pass through three more full carriages of reclining seats before finally reaching the dining carriage.

At the entrance, Daphne approaches the maître d' in his black uniform. "Five for dinner, please," she says.

"Welcome, ladies and gentlemen," says the maître d'. "I apologize. I cannot seat all five of you at a single table. It is customary to share tables with fellow passengers."

"We don't mind," says Daphne. "We love meeting new people."

Turn the page.

The maître d' ushers the gang between booths with white tablecloths and classy silverware. He seats Daphne, Velma, and Fred with a skinny man with spiky blonde hair. Scooby and Shaggy are seated across the aisle with a man and woman who look alike. Both have rectangular faces and black hair and blue eyes. "Your waiter will be with you shortly," the maître d' says.

"*Ciao!*" the woman chirps to Shaggy and Scooby. "Hello." She has a cheerful Italian accent. "I am Rosa Robbiolo, and this is my brother, Roberto."

"Hello," Roberto says in a deep voice.

"Hi," Shaggy replies, tucking his napkin into his shirt. "I'm Shaggy, and this is Scooby-Doo."

Scooby lifts his paw to shake Rosa's hand.

"Are you travelling to the cheese convention, too?" asks Rosa.

"Nope," answers Shaggy. "We're checking out the sights. But a cheese convention sounds like somewhere we should go, right, Scoobs?"

"Rou ret!" says Scooby.

Shaggy picks up the menu. "So," he asks, "are you going to this convention to taste cheese?"

"I am entered in a contest for the greatest cheese," replies Roberto. "I created a mozzarella so creamy it makes strong men weep with joy."

"The prize is one million dollars," adds Rosa. "With many more millions in sales afterward."

"Zoinks!" exclaims Shaggy.

"It has taken me twenty years to perfect the recipe," says Roberto. "It is my life's work. This will be the greatest honour of my career."

"Roberto is a cheese genius," says his sister.

"Forget it, Chef Robbiolo!" cries the man with spiky blonde hair across the aisle. The scrawny Frenchman leans past Velma to sneer at Roberto. "The Cheese Cup is mine! My Muenster cheese will win the trophy . . . along with the million!"

"Chef Georges Fromage," Roberto replies, "you're insane. Nobody gives a prize to Muenster cheese over mozzarella."

Turn the page.

Georges says, "Mozzarella is a bland cheese."

"Your annoying personality prevents you from winning anything," Roberto says. "You are a second-rate cheesemaker."

"I'll show you!" Georges cries, his face turning red. "I'll win! Someday the name Fromage will mean 'cheese' across the world!"

"Wait," says Velma. "Doesn't *fromage* already mean 'cheese'?"

"Rival chefs!" another man interrupts, calling from a table a few booths away. "How delicious." He stands, a portly man with a handlebar moustache, grinning at Roberto and Georges. "I love serious competition."

Scooby's eyes widen when a tiny monkey lands on the man's shoulder and curls his tail around the man's fleshy neck. The monkey wears a red vest with brass buttons.

"Who are you?" demands Roberto.

"What?" shrieks Georges. "Truly, you do not recognize the King of Cheese?"

"Ruh?" gasps Scooby.

"Yes!" says Georges. "Alexander Iskender here is the most important cheese merchant. He can make your cheese famous throughout Europe!"

Roberto's face pales. *"Signore* Iskender," he says, "my apologies for not recognizing you and your famous monkey, Zips. It is an honour to be travelling on the same train."

"Don't let it go to your head, Robbiolo," says Alexander. "You cannot make friends with me so that I will sell your cheese."

"I would never play games to hype my creation!" Roberto insists. "My mozzarella is pure, milky beauty."

"So show me," Alexander says. The monkey laughs. "Give me a sneak peek of your marvellous mozzarella."

"That is against the rules!" cries Georges.

"No, it is not," replies Alexander. "I am not a judge, merely a merchant interested in selling good cheese."

Turn the page.

"Fine," agrees Roberto. "You may glimpse my mozzarella. Let's go."

Roberto and Rosa slide out of the booth and march towards the kitchen carriage. Alexander and his monkey follow the Italian brother and sister.

"Excuse me, please," Georges says to Velma, and she gets up, letting him into the aisle. The French chef rushes after the others.

"Should we go, too?" Velma asks. "I'm curious about the cheese competition."

"But, like, we haven't eaten," complains Shaggy. "Let's stay here."

"Reah, Ri'm rungry," says Scooby.

"I vote we go," says Fred. "I smell a cheesy mystery."

"So, Daphne?" asks Velma. "You're the tie-breaker."

"Hmm," says Daphne.

If Daphne decides that they should go and peek at the cheese, turn to page 20.

If Daphne chooses to stay and eat dinner, turn to page 90.

Fred glances in both directions out of the window. The train is passing through a flat, marshy landscape, and there are no tunnels ahead. To the left, he sees the thin metal rungs of a ladder leading onto the roof.

The gremlin scurries up the last rung and disappears over the top.

"We've got to catch it," Fred declares. He grabs the nearest rung and climbs up the ladder. Velma, Daphne, Scooby, and then Shaggy follow him. The wind whips at their hair and clothes as they climb, and the scenery whizzes by in a blur.

When they reach the top, they stand in a careful crouch, holding onto each other.

The gremlin stands at the edge of the carriage, facing the front of the train, with the engine far ahead. "Like, this is so dangerous," says Shaggy.

"Reah," agrees Scooby. "Roo rangerous!"

Turn to 44.

The luggage carriage is dark when the gang enters to look for Georges. Fred shines his torch over the metal racks of suitcases and boxes.

"Like, it's spooky in here with the lights off," says Shaggy.

Scooby's teeth chatter. "Reah," he agrees. "Rooky."

"Doesn't it feel different since we were last here?" asks Velma. "I have a hunch things were moved around, but I can't tell where or what."

Daphne runs a finger along a steamer trunk. "Someone could hide easily in these," she whispers, "especially someone as skinny as Georges Fromage."

"Maybe someone tampered with the safe," suggests Fred. "We could inspect it again."

"Or we could look through the luggage," says Daphne.

"I don't know," says Velma. "The luggage is the passengers' private property."

If the gang examines the safe, turn to page 74.

If they take a closer look at the luggage, turn to page 77.

The gang rushes out of the dining car and through the kitchen corridor. With a lurch, the train starts chugging and rolling again, causing them to crash into the steel cooking compartment's wall before continuing to run.

Shaggy glances back.

The enormous rat is in hot pursuit, squealing with its claws outstretched.

"Hurry!" cries Shaggy. "It's gaining on us!"

When they hurtle into the observation carriage, the train pulls out of the tunnel. Outside, on either side of the elevated track trestle, rolling fields are dotted with little haystack hills.

The other passengers shriek at the huge rat.

Scooby trips. He gets tangled in his friends, and they roll in a ball against the glass wall. Trying to slow their spin, Fred grabs a lever – but it's the handle for the emergency door, which pops open.

The gang tumbles off the train, screaming.

Turn to page 37

In Alexander's private stateroom, Daphne hurries to pick up the cardboard box that fell from the luggage rack. "I'm curious about what's in here," she says. "I have a hunch it's important."

"Rit's reese," replies Scooby, sniffing. "Rozzarella!"

Daphne takes the lid off the box. "He's right!" she says, showing the pure-white, milky cheese to the others. "It's the missing million-dollar mozzarella!"

"Mmm-mmm!" moans Scooby, sniffing closer and deeper. He starts drooling.

"Yeah, Scoobs," says Shaggy. "It sure does smell good." He reaches for the cheese. "Maybe we could just have a tiny taste."

Velma steps in front of the box of stolen cheese. "No way," she says. "We should turn it in to the authorities. It's our proof that Alexander is the thief!"

If the gang reports Alexander to the authorities, turn to page 34.

If they taste a tiny piece of cheese, turn to page 56.

"I want to see a million-dollar mozzarella," says Daphne.

After some half-hearted, hungry grumbling by Shaggy and Scooby, the gang hurries out of the dining carriage.

They squeeze through the small kitchen carriage, alongside a gleaming steel compartment where cooks are making dinner. After cruising through the observation carriage – its curved-window walls and ceiling showing the full gorgeous landscape outside – they catch up with the cheese crowd outside the luggage carriage.

Georges holds the door for the gang. They slip past him into the stacked rows of suitcases inside the dim space.

With a wave of his hand, Roberto ushers the group along the carriage. At the end, he leans over to an electronic keypad on an enormous metal safe.

Roberto sticks out his tongue as he pushes buttons awkwardly. He turns the handle on the safe.

Turn to page 58.

The police catch Alexander in the kitchen carriage. The shorter officer leaps and grabs his ankle. Alexander falls on his face. He lets go of the ball of mozzarella he was holding.

Zips scrambles for the rolling ball, but Scooby reaches it first.

Chef Roberto grabs the cheese and hugs it. "My mozzarella!" he sobs.

"As I suspected," says Velma, "Alexander took the cheese. He could make millions from that stolen mozzarella."

"I would've got away with it, too," says Alexander, "if it hadn't been for you kids!"

After the police take away Alexander and Zips, Roberto hugs everyone. "Thank you!" he gushes. "When I win the competition, I will send you a lifetime supply of my finest mozzarella!"

"For rife?!" says Scooby. He giggles, thrilled.

The gang laughs, congratulating themselves on solving the case of the cheese thief.

THE END

To follow another path, turn to page 14.

"We're climbing up the milk tank," Fred decides.

Carefully, everyone follows Fred up the rungs of the ladder. The wind whips at them as they step along the top of the curved tank towards the valve in the middle.

"Should I open it?" asks Fred.

"Like, why not?" replies Shaggy nervously. "We've come this far!"

Fred flips the latch on the circular valve.

It pops open violently. The tank was pressurized, so the milk gushes out in a white, cold geyser. The creamy milk blasts right into the gang, hosing them off the top of the tank.

All five of them, soaked in chilly milk, tumble off the train.

Turn to page 35.

The Mystery Inc. gang searches for Rosa and Roberto Robbiolo, pushing through many carriages towards the front of the train. Finally they spot the Italian brother and sister outside a sleeper compartment.

"Why do we not call the police?" Roberto asks Rosa. "Each second we delay, it is more difficult to find my magnificent mozzarella."

"The cheese is on the train," replies Rosa. "The thief will make a mistake and reveal himself–"

"Like, any idea who that thief is?" asks Shaggy.

"How rude to interrupt me!" says Rosa. "Do you have no manners?"

Shaggy blushes while Scooby giggles.

"We're sorry to interrupt," says Velma, "but do you mind if we ask you a few questions?"

Turn to page 29.

Fred dives at the gremlin.

The gremlin dodges left, avoiding capture. It scrambles up one curved wall, bounces off the ceiling corner, and ricochets across the sofa before scurrying towards the curtained window.

Velma jumps in front of the creature, blocking it from escape. The gremlin grabs onto Velma's skirt and climbs up her clothing with its claws. It leaps off her shoulder, soaring above Shaggy and Scooby, and crashes into the lamp.

The lounge plunges into darkness.

Great-Aunt Ida screams, "We are doomed!"

"Relp!" moans Scooby.

The gang hears one of the lounge doors opening . . . and closing.

Fred fumbles for his torch, but he finds no sign of the gremlin in either direction.

"Which way did it go?" asks Daphne.

If the gang looks for the gremlin towards the guard's van, turn to page 64.

If they think it went towards the stateroom, turn to page 79.

"We believe you," Daphne says, handing Georges her handkerchief.

Georges sits up and blows his nose.

"It'd be better if you had proof," says Velma. "Where were you when the cheese was stolen?"

"I don't know exactly when the mozzarella was taken," says Georges, "but for hours before dinner, I was in the kitchen carriage, arguing with the cook about his cheese. He can confirm!"

The gang follows Georges into the kitchen carriage, and they knock on the door of the metal compartment.

The cook opens the door and groans when he sees Georges. "You again!"

"Was he here this afternoon?" asks Fred.

"All day this man pesters me!" the cook thunders. "Nobody wants Muenster on their pizza! It is madness!"

"People want Muenster pizza!" says Georges.

"Huh," says Velma. "He told the truth."

Turn to page 65.

"Hi, Rosa," says Fred cheerfully. "Do you play cards often?"

Rosa shrugs. "Often enough," she replies. "Would you care to challenge me to a game of blackjack?"

"Sure," says Fred. He sits down in a chair across from Rosa. "If I win, will you answer a few questions?"

Rosa laughs. "You're not going to win." She expertly deals the cards. "Twenty-one!" she exclaims, pointing to a queen and ace in front of her. "I win. See? Would anyone else like to try?"

"I'll give it a go," says Daphne. She takes Fred's place.

After the first deal, Daphne has a seven and a nine. "Hit me," she says.

Rosa deals her a king. "Twenty-six," she says. "Bust. I win again."

"My luck is usually better than that," says Daphne with a sigh.

"Anyone else?" asks Rosa.

Turn to page 49.

"Thanks," cheers Shaggy. "I'm famished!"

Alexander cuts some cheese for Shaggy.

Shaggy gobbles it down. Fred tries a piece, although Velma and Daphne decline politely. Scooby eats two slices, licking his lips.

"Rummy!" says Scooby.

Then Shaggy's stomach churns. He presses his hands to his sides, groaning.

"Mr Iskender," asks Fred, "where were you before you went to the dining carriage earlier?"

"My dear boy," says Alexander, "you don't really suspect me, do you?"

"Well–" Fred's face turns green.

"Are you all right?" asks Alexander.

"No," says Fred. "I don't feel so good."

"Ree reither!" moans Scooby.

"Where's the bathroom?" begs Shaggy.

"In the guard's van," says Alexander. He points to the far door. "Through there!"

Turn to page 48.

"You kids with your questions!" says Rosa. "We are stressed, and you meddle in our lives."

"They are trying to help," says Roberto.

"Now you interrupt me, too?" demands Rosa. "I have done nothing in our entire lives except help you achieve your mozzarella dreams. This is how you repay me, with rudeness? I tend your precious cattle, oversee their milking, manage transportation, and protect you from the ghost cow haunting this train–"

"Rhost row!" cries Scooby.

"Another interruption!" screams Rosa.

"You didn't protect my mozzarella that well," says Roberto. "Now it is stolen."

Rosa glares at her brother. "You are impossible!" she shouts, stomping out of the sleeper carriage towards the front of the train.

"I will find the mozzarella myself!" yells Roberto, and he storms in the opposite direction.

If the gang follows Rosa, turn to page 54.
If they tail Roberto, turn to page 101.

The gang returns to the fancy lounge.

Alexander and Great-Aunt Ida munch on mouldy cheese. "Not everyone can handle the Aglöö," says Alexander.

Zips bounces on Alexander's shoulder.

"Mr Iskender," says Velma, "couldn't the stolen mozzarella make you a lot of money?"

"I am not interested in selling Robbiolo's mozzarella," says Alexander. "I have a source already – my cousin is a cheese chef, too."

"Small Abraham," croaks Great-Aunt Ida.

"Yes," agrees Alexander. "Her grandson is a promising chef. Abe made this Aglöö."

"So," asks Fred, "Chef Robbiolo being out of the contest would help Abe's business?"

Alexander raises an objecting finger . . . but he gulps. His face turns green. "Excuse me." He flees with Zips on his shoulder.

"That cheese is dangerous," says Daphne.

"Aglöö," says Great-Aunt Ida, smiling.

Turn to page 76.

"It's clear that you didn't steal your brother's mozzarella," Velma tells Rosa.

"I'm glad that is all straightened out," Rosa replies.

"So, like, we're back to square one," says Shaggy.

"Excuse me, Ms Robbiolo," asks Daphne, "who do you think is the cheese thief, Georges Fromage . . . or Alexander Iskender?"

"You want my opinion?" asks Rosa.

"We'd love to know what you think," says Fred.

"All right," says Rosa. "I've never liked that Fromage person. I think he stole the cheese."

"That's very possible," says Velma, "but I'm not sure. Alexander Iskender has lots of reasons to steal your brother's cheese, too."

"It certainly could be the King of Cheese," Rosa agrees, "but my money's on Fromage."

If the gang turns their attention to Georges Fromage, turn to page 97.

If they now investigate Alexander Iskender, turn to page 36.

"Like, let go!" shouts Shaggy. He gives the cheese another strong pull.

Georges drops his end of the mozzarella. The cheese snaps like a rubber band, and the gang gets flung through the open emergency exit.

They all shriek as they tumble outside, the cheese flinging in loops around them as they fall.

One loop of the super-stretchy mozzarella is still tangled around the pole. The cheese retracts, and the gang gets trapped inside a cobweb of sticky strands, dangling high above the mountains on the pole.

Georges waves goodbye from the observation carriage. The departing train leaves the Mystery Inc. gang snarled in a net of million-dollar mozzarella string cheese.

THE END

To follow another path, turn to page 14.

The gang pushes out of Alexander's stateroom into the luggage carriage. Inside, they find two uniformed Swiss police officers inspecting the safe with Roberto and Rosa Robbiolo.

"We were looking for you," Shaggy tells them.

Both policemen stand up straight and glare meanly at the gang. "Why?" demands the shorter one. "Are you confessing to committing a crime?"

"Ruh?" asks Scooby.

"Confess?" blurts Shaggy. "We didn't do anything wrong! I don't think . . ."

"You look suspicious to us," says the tall cop.

Velma adds, "We've been trying to help."

"They have been very interested in my missing mozzarella," says Roberto.

"Too interested," adds Rosa.

"These officers don't seem very nice," whispers Daphne. "I'm not sure I trust them."

"Me neither," replies Fred.

If the gang hides the cheese from the police, turn to page 40.
If they reveal the stolen mozzarella, turn to page 47.

The gang falls towards a pasture below the train tracks, screaming as they plummet down the hill.

"Like, watch out for the cows!" shouts Shaggy, propelling his arms so he doesn't bash into the cattle below.

Instead of hitting cows, Fred, Velma, Daphne, Shaggy, and Scooby all land in a huge pile of stinking mud. The gunk breaks their fall, but smells absolutely horrible.

Scooby holds his nose and gags.

As the gang tries to wade out of the gross pile of goo, the train keeps rolling along the tracks.

Roberto pokes his head out of a window in the cattle carriage. He waves goodbye as the train rumbles out of view over the horizon.

THE END

To follow another path, turn to page 14.

The gang heads to the guard's van, near where they last saw Alexander and Zips. Attached to the luggage carriage is a fancy wooden carriage. On the door, the word *Private* is written.

Fred knocks. "Mr Iskender?"

Alexander opens the door. "Ah," he says, "the investigating teenagers. Please come in." He ushers them into an old-fashioned stateroom with brass decor and velvet wallpaper. A bed along one side is folded up into a sofa.

"Welcome," says Alexander. "I often travel by train, so I attach my own carriages and enjoy comfort."

"That's how to live," says Daphne. "May we ask a few–?"

"Questions?" finishes Alexander. "Certainly, but not here. It's more comfortable in my lounge carriage." He whistles a series of trills.

Zips repeats the whistle exactly and leaps onto Alexander's shoulder.

They lead the gang into the next carriage.

Turn to page 66.

It's a long, frightening fall from the high train trestle into the farm below.

Scooby, Shaggy, Velma, Fred, and Daphne windmill their arms as they plunge down. One by one, they land in plump, mounded haystacks of straw.

Daphne struggles to the top of her haystack, spitting straw out of her mouth. "Ugh," she cries. "It's not as soft as it looks!"

"It itches all over," says Velma, rubbing her arms.

"Look!" shouts Fred. He points up at the departing train.

In the open emergency door of the observation carriage, Georges Fromage hangs outside a little. He's wearing a rat costume and holding the giant rat head under his arm.

Georges grins and waves goodbye to the members of Mystery Inc. as the train disappears into the distance.

THE END

To follow another path, turn to page 14.

The conductor strides into the luggage carriage. He sees the gang huddled on the floor. "You're probably safest in here, kids. The tunnel has collapsed. We need to back up. Hang on!"

The floor jolts. The horrible sound of scraping metal vibrates around them as the train reverses through the rock rubble. The conductor joins the gang in their tight, frightened knot.

After a slow, screeching roll backwards, the train stops.

"We're out," says the conductor. He leads the gang to the guard's van, where they exit and join a crowd of evacuated passengers in a stony field.

"This train's not going anywhere," the conductor announces. "Buses will arrive shortly to take you to the nearest town."

Scooby lets out a groan.

The train trip is over.

Mystery Inc. never discovers who stole the million-dollar mozzarella.

THE END

To follow another path, turn to page 14.

"You may ask," replies Georges, "but I cannot promise an answer."

"When Chef Robbiolo's mozzarella was missing," asks Velma, "why did you smile?"

"Because I'm a naturally happy person?" answers Georges. He looks worried.

"Try again," says Daphne.

"I am guilty!" Georges cries.

"You stole the mozzarella?" asks Fred.

Georges widens his teary eyes. "No," he insists. "Only a terrible person would be thrilled about Robbiolo's misfortune. I was gleeful because I am jealous! It's my lifelong dream for Muenster to get respect. Just once, I'd love to see Muenster on a pizza instead of mozzarella!"

He burrows his face into Scooby's furry shoulder, sobbing. Scooby pats his back.

"I believe him," Daphne proclaims.

"I'm not so sure," says Velma.

If the gang trusts Georges's story, turn to page 26.
If they decide he's lying, turn to page 61.

Fred hides the mozzarella behind his back.

Rosa spots the edge of the box around him. "What's that you're holding there?" she asks.

"Show us," insists the shorter officer. The taller policeman steps around Fred and pulls the box out of his hands.

"It's my missing mozzarella!" cries Roberto. "These kids stole it!"

"We didn't!" Velma protests. "We found the box . . . in Alexander Iskender's stateroom!"

"How dare you insult the King of Cheese!" thunders the taller policeman.

"You have no proof," says the shorter officer. "Why would you hide the mozzarella if you're innocent? You're under arrest!"

So Chef Robbiolo gets his mozzarella back . . . but the Mystery Inc. gang is hauled into the Geneva police station and questioned for hours.

Eventually they are released, but Alexander is never brought to justice.

THE END

To follow another path, turn to page 14.

The cattle carriage is dark and spooky. The cows shift around in their pens, moaning weird sounds.

"Like, I don't like this at all," whispers Shaggy.

"Reah," agrees Scooby with a shudder.

"Keep it together," hisses Daphne, but she sounds a little scared, too.

Fred peers over the edge of a pen. He sees a normal-looking cow contentedly chewing its cud. "Nothing weird here," he says.

Suddenly a loud thump echoes through the cattle carriage. The cows all shift around nervously.

"What . . . like, what was that noise?" asks Shaggy.

Velma huddles near her friends and points deeper into the carriage. "It came from over there," she says.

Turn to page 62.

Roberto and Rosa shift away from the safe so that Fred can kneel down beside it.

Velma peers over Fred's shoulder.

Fred shines a penlight into the safe's boxy interior. "Let's see what we've got here," he says.

"This is an unnecessary investigation," says Alexander, petting his monkey under the chin. "Chef Robbiolo simply took the cheese out earlier and forgot where he put it."

"Nonsense!" argues Roberto. "I did not lose my cheese willy-nilly! I have not seen it since Rosa locked the safe."

"What's this?" asks Fred. He picks up a thread and hands it to Velma, who puts it in a plastic bag. Velma holds it up, and everybody stares at the red thread.

"It's the same colour as Rosa's scarf," says Daphne.

"Or Roberto's tie," says Fred.

"The thread fell in when I locked up the cheese," says Rosa. "It is not a serious clue."

Turn to page 70.

"Grab that gremlin!" shouts Fred.

The gremlin shrieks and hops to the next carriage, scampering along the top of the train.

The members of Mystery Inc. jump across the gap, too, racing after the gremlin. Fred catches up quickly and tackles the critter.

The gremlin sprawls flat. A rubber mask pops off, revealing a tiny monkey underneath.

"Like, look!" says Shaggy. "It's Zips!"

"Rips!" repeats Scooby, surprised.

Zips screeches and squirms out of Fred's grasp. He swiftly dodges through the others' attempts to grab him. In the middle of the carriage, Zips zooms towards the ladder . . . and scurries onto the shoulder of the King of Cheese, who is climbing up to the top.

Alexander Iskender wears a black cape. His eyes glint with cold menace.

If the gang runs away along the train top, turn to page 72.
If they rush at Alexander and Zips, turn to page 88.

Shaggy quickly whistles a cheery little tune, trying to coax the gremlin back into the stateroom.

For a long moment, nothing happens. Everybody stands around the window quietly and waits.

Daphne says, "I think it's gone!"

A sharply whistled tune floats in the window. It's Shaggy's melody exactly. The gremlin stays hidden from sight on the outside of the speeding train.

"Try another whistle," suggests Velma.

"Or," Fred whispers, "now that we've found the gremlin, we could try to grab it."

If they climb out the window and chase the gremlin, turn to page 15.

If Shaggy whistles another tune, turn to page 87.

"Explain the rat costume," says Velma.

"Okay," sobs Georges. "Remember I told you of my jealousy for mozzarella? How my true desire is to see Muenster cheese on pizza all over the world?"

"More or less," says Fred.

"Well, this train's cooks denied me!" Georges cries. "I begged them to make Muenster pizza, but they refused. So I dressed up like a rat to scare their customers. It is foolish, but that's what I did."

"So, like, you didn't steal the mozzarella?" asks Shaggy.

"Never!" replies Georges. "I may be obsessed with Muenster, but I am not a thief."

"I believe him," says Daphne.

"I'm not so sure," says Velma. "I still think we should let the police decide."

If the gang believes Georges's explanation, turn to page 99.
If they bring him to the authorities, turn to page 51.

Despite the officers' bad attitude, Velma takes the box from Fred and hands it to the shorter policeman. "Sir," she says, "we found this in Alexander Iskender's stateroom. I think you'll find the contents interesting."

"Really rinteresting," adds Scooby.

As the officer opens the box, Alexander enters the luggage carriage with Zips on his shoulder. "My box!" he cries, shocked.

Immediately Alexander realizes he has said too much. He claps his hand over his mouth. Then he jumps forward and grabs the cheese in both hands. With Zips screeching in rage, Alexander turns and flees the luggage carriage.

"The King of Cheese stole my mozzarella!" shouts Roberto. "Officers, get him!"

Turn to page 21.

Fred, Shaggy, and Scooby race through the door and barrel into the three bathrooms they find at the front of the guard's van.

Velma and Daphne follow and wait in the guard's van's narrow hall.

The boys feel better quickly, once the toxic Aglöö is out of them. They exit the toilets sheepishly.

"That'll teach you to not eat everything put in front of you," says Velma.

"It tasted pretty good," moans Shaggy. "Going down, at least."

"Reah," groans Scooby-Doo.

"Gross," says Daphne. "So . . . what should we do now? Go back into Alexander's lounge or look around this guard's van?" She peers down the hall into the dim space beyond the toilets.

"It would be rude to keep Alexander waiting," says Velma. "Plus I still have questions for him."

If the gang returns to Alexander's lounge, turn to page 30.
If they investigate the guard's van, turn to page 82.

"I'll play," says Velma, "but you seem awfully good at playing cards. I'm not sure blackjack is my game, either."

"Anything you wish to play, I will play," replies Rosa.

"Same stakes?" asks Velma. "If I win, you'll answer some questions?"

"I have not agreed to any stakes," says Rosa, "but I will play."

"Play a board game!" says Shaggy. "Like, those are the best."

"Ronopoly," suggests Scooby.

"You could always play go fish," jokes Daphne.

"Hmm," says Velma. "I'm not sure."

"Decide quickly," says Rosa, "or I will return to playing patience."

If Velma challenges Rosa to a card game, turn to page 78.

If she chooses a board game, turn to page 57.

"Let's ask the cooks if they've seen Georges," says Fred.

The kitchen carriage smells delicious. Shaggy and Scooby drool in the corridor outside.

Velma knocks on the door.

An angry cook sticks her head out. "What?" she asks. "We're cooking without power here!"

"Pardon," replies Daphne. "Have you seen Chef Fromage?"

"Who?" the cook asks.

"A skinny cheese dude?" answers Shaggy. "With, like, spiky blonde hair, or wearing a beret?"

"The Muenster maniac?" says the cook. "He's mad, trying to stop us from putting mozzarella on our pizza. He rushed to the dining carriage."

Then the cook slams the door.

"Rude!" says Daphne. "I think she's pulling our leg. Let's search the luggage room instead."

If the gang takes the cook's advice and searches the dining carriage, turn to page 52.

If they head back to the luggage carriage, turn to page 77.

Fred and Shaggy hold onto Georges's arms.

"Let go!" cries Georges. "I'm innocent!"

"The police will decide that," says Velma.

The gang drags Georges towards the locomotive. They find two Swiss police officers.

"We caught the cheese thief!" Daphne announces. "Here he is."

The two officers blink in surprise. "That's not the thief," says the shorter officer. "We already have a full confession from the real culprit."

"You do?" gasps Shaggy. "Like, who?"

"I don't see how that's your business," the taller officer says. He glares at the gang. "A false accusation is a serious crime. We'll need to take you kids into the station for questioning."

"But I didn't do anything," sneers Georges.

At the next stop, the police escort the gang from the train . . . and send them home. Their European train adventure is over.

THE END

To follow another path, turn to page 14.

The gang steps into the dining carriage and finds total chaos. They can't see far into the carriage because of the panicked passengers scrambling around screaming in the narrow space. Plates, cutlery, and food litter the floor.

"What is going on?" blurts Fred.

Two older women hop onto a table and shriek. One points down the aisle.

Shaggy peers over the crowd. "It's a . . . giant rat!" he yells. "Like, the size of a man!"

The enormous rat saunters through the throng. It has a huge head and razor-sharp teeth. It walks on its hind legs. It raises its claws and threatens a little boy in a booth.

The boy bursts into tears.

"Leave him alone!" yells Fred.

"Let's catch this rat," says Velma.

"Are you nuts?" cries Shaggy. "Run away!"

If the gang tackles the giant rat, turn to page 105.
If they flee, turn to page 17.

In the front of the train, the gang gathers around Rosa in the games room.

"Rosa," Daphne asks softly, "may we please talk to you?"

Rosa nods. "You said 'please,'" she says. "At least one of you has manners."

"Thank you," replies Daphne. "I'm sorry to suspect you stole your brother's cheese, but you did have access to the safe. We could rule you out completely if you had an alibi."

"Ralibi," agrees Scooby-Doo.

"That's all you want?" asks Rosa. She brings them over to a small table where four old women play cards.

"Rosa," the oldest lady says, "come and play with us again."

"When did she play last?" asks Velma.

"All afternoon," replies the ancient woman. "We played bridge for hours before dinner."

Rosa smiles.

Turn to page 31.

The gang finds two Swiss police officers with Roberto and Rosa Robbiolo in the luggage carriage. At the same time, Alexander Iskender and Zips enter from the other side.

"Hello," Roberto greets everyone sadly. "We are still searching for my cheese. You haven't found it, have you?"

"We've got a good lead," says Velma. "Would you mind playing the musical code again?"

Rosa plays the notes for the safe's code.

"Whistle it," Velma tells Shaggy.

Shaggy whistles the little tune . . . and Zips whistles it back exactly.

Everyone stares at Zips in shock.

"That's how Alexander learned the safe code!" Velma crows. "He had his monkey hide in here and memorize it!"

"You'll never take me alive!" screams Alexander. He and Zips bolt out of the luggage carriage, with the police hot on their heels.

Turn to page 21.

"That is the most delicious cheese I've ever smelled," says Daphne. "Maybe tasting one little chunk wouldn't hurt."

Fred peers into the box. "A few crumbs have fallen off," he replies. "We could taste those."

"Fine," grumbles Velma. "I'm curious myself. It does have an amazing aroma." She pinches a morsel of mozzarella from the bottom of the box and pops it in her mouth. "Mmm," she moans.

Daphne, Fred, and Shaggy try teeny crumbs of cheese. They act like it's the best cheese they've ever tasted in their lives.

Scooby gives his crumb a little lick. The mozzarella is unbelievably yummy. He gobbles the chunk and swallows. His eyes swirl in wild delight.

"Ruh-roh," Scooby says. He grabs the whole ball of cheese and holds it, drooling.

"No, no, Scoobs," warns Shaggy. "Like, put that back in the box."

Turn to page 84.

"We'll play a board game," Velma decides. She peers at the bookshelf filled with game boxes.

The old ladies across the carriage never look up from their card game.

"Ronopoly!" insists Scooby.

Velma brings the Monopoly box to the table. She lifts the lid. Inside, somewhat squished, is a piece of the missing million-dollar mozzarella!

Everyone cries out in amazement.

"Rosa must've hidden it," says Fred. "Let's get the police!"

"Like, if she knew it was there," argues Shaggy, "she wouldn't agree to play Monopoly! Let's ask her."

Scooby sniffs the mozzarella. He starts drooling uncontrollably.

If the gang accuses Rosa of stealing the cheese, turn to page 71.

If they ask Rosa how it got in the box, turn to page 81.

If Scooby tastes the mozzarella, turn to page 84.

The safe door doesn't open. "What a difficult thing!" Roberto swears.

"Again you forget the code," says Rosa. "Here, move, let me do it."

She reaches around her brother and types a short song of beeps on the keypad.

When Roberto pulls the handle, the lock clicks and the safe door opens a crack.

Roberto turns to face everybody. "Inside is the future of cheese!" he declares. "Behold my million-dollar mozzarella!"

He pulls the safe door fully open. Rosa gasps in shock. Roberto glances inside and bellows like a bull. His face turns dark red.

The safe is completely empty.

"Robbiolo," says Alexander the merchant, "is this your idea of a bad joke?"

"No!" screams Roberto. "Someone has stolen my cheese!"

If Fred offers to help find the missing mozzarella, turn to page 68.

If the gang decides to avoid this cheese drama, turn to page 90.

Velma squares her shoulders and faces the ghost cow hurtling towards the gang.

Fred can't let her attack the monster alone, so he stands beside her. When the ghost cow gets close enough, Fred and Velma jump at it . . . and grab its front legs.

The ghost cow topples over in a heap. One of its shoes pops off.

It's a blue high heel.

"That's Rosa's!" exclaims Daphne.

With a loud sigh, the cow pulls the head off its costume. Inside is Rosa, looking annoyed. "Okay," she grumbles. "You got us."

"Rus?" asks Scooby.

The ghost cow splits in two, revealing Roberto in the costume's back half. He looks abashed.

"Give us a chance to explain," says Rosa.

"Your guilt seems pretty obvious to me!" replies Daphne.

If the gang hears the Robbiolos' explanation, turn to page 89.

If they drag Rosa to the police, turn to page 71.

Fred raises his hands in surrender and slowly takes a step backward.

The gremlin screeches in laughter. It takes Fred's backing away as a sign of weakness – and it attacks! The green critter scrambles at Fred, slashing with its claws.

Fred scoots back further, just missing getting scratched.

"Like, get out of there, Fred!" yells Shaggy from the gang's tangle on the floor.

"Reah!" says Scooby. "Run raway!"

Velma sits up and pushes Scooby off of her. "Just grab that gremlin!" she shouts. "It's only a foot tall!"

"No!" cries Daphne. "Let's escape this crazy carriage!"

If Fred follows Velma's advice and tries to catch the gremlin, turn to page 25.

If the gang runs out of the lounge, turn to page 98.

Velma says, "His jealousy of mozzarella makes him more likely to steal his competition."

Daphne throws an arm around the sobbing French cheese chef. "But look how sad Georges is," she replies.

"I'm sorry," says Velma, "but I don't think he's being completely honest."

"Rook!" cries Scooby-Doo. "Ra runnel!"

The gang peers through the glass ceiling of the observation carriage at a tall, snow-covered mountain looming above. The train rushes into a dark tunnel, dimming the carriage all around. Soft white lights under the benches glow faintly, keeping the carriage illuminated.

"Like," wonders Shaggy nervously, "how deep does this train go under the mountain–?"

With a sharp shock, the train lurches as it stops abruptly in the tunnel. Everybody tumbles off the padded benches. The lights go out.

Shaggy and Scooby scream along with the other passengers in total darkness.

Turn to page 94.

A huge glowing cow stands up at the end of the carriage. It waves its front legs and moans horribly.

Shaggy's hair stands on end. "The ghost cow!" he shrieks.

The terrifying cow spectre hurtles down the aisle towards the gang. All their eyes are wide and scared in the ghost cow's eerie glow.

"I'm outta here!" screams Shaggy. He turns to run, with Scooby right by his side.

"Wait!" yells Velma. "That can't be real. There's no such thing as a ghost cow."

"Like, use your eyes!" shouts Shaggy. "There's a ghost cow right in front of you . . . and it's coming to get us!"

If the gang flees in terror, turn to page **96**.

If they try to tackle the ghost cow, turn to page **59**.

The gang rushes out of the lounge carriage towards the guard's van. The sound of the wind rushing by the train outside is much louder in the space between carriages.

"Wait!" calls Velma. She points at a small hole in the rubber accordion that encloses the connecting area, above the closed exit door. "Maybe the gremlin crawled through there, up onto the roof."

"It could be an old hole," says Daphne. "The gremlin could have continued into the guard's van instead."

"Or, like, maybe it didn't come in this direction," suggests Shaggy. "Maybe it went into the stateroom the other way, after all."

"We can't let it escape," says Fred.

If the gang checks inside the guard's van, turn to page **82.**

If they backtrack to the stateroom, turn to page **79.**

If they open the train door and see if the gremlin climbed onto the roof, turn to page **15.**

"So, like, if Chef Fromage is innocent," asks Shaggy, "we should stop investigating him, right?"

"Reah," says Scooby.

"Yes," agrees Velma. "Let's cross Georges off our list of suspects."

"Who should we follow instead?" asks Daphne. "Rosa Robbiolo, Chef Roberto's sister? Or the King of Cheese, Alexander Iskender?"

"Rosa had access to the cheese safe," says Fred. "Let's find out what she knows."

"But I've got a hunch about Alexander," says Velma. "Let's go talk to him."

If the gang investigates Rosa Robbiolo, turn to page 24.

If they switch their attention to Alexander Iskender, turn to page 36.

Alexander's lounge is as luxurious as his stateroom. A bar, bookshelves, armchairs, and a sofa surround tables bolted to the floor. The curtains on the windows are drawn – the only light comes from a large shaded lamp. On one of the armchairs, an old lady perches, doing a puzzle.

"This is my Great-Aunt Ida," says Iskender. "She travels with me, but speaks little English." Aunt Ida raises her teacup in greeting and sips.

"What country are you from originally?" asks Velma.

"An Adriatic island that no longer exists," replies Alexander. "It sank. We were famous for our delicious Aglöö cheese." He crosses to a table and raises a glass dome off a serving tray, revealing a bright blue wedge of cheese.

Scooby sniffs. The Aglöö cheese smells strongly of feet.

"Would you like to try?" asks Alexander.

If the gang tries the cheese, turn to page 28.
If they decline Alexander's offer, turn to page 91.

Scooby-Doo leans left – and successfully blocks the mouse.

The mouse squeals in anger. It spits the cheese at Scooby.

Scooby catches the cheese on the edge of his lips.

The mouse takes the opportunity of Scooby being distracted to run between his legs and escape out the hole in the door.

Meanwhile, Scooby gets a whiff of the chunk of mozzarella he's holding between his lips.

It smells so incredibly delicious.

Scooby breaks out in a sweat.

He must taste the mozzarella!

Turn to page 84.

"Chef Robbiolo," says Fred, "we're a group called Mystery Inc. We have a terrific track record solving mysteries just like this one."

Roberto grabs onto Fred's arm. "Thank goodness you're here!" he says as Fred helps him to his feet. "If I don't bring that cheese to the convention, I'll lose the most important competition of my life!"

"Oh, you were going to lose to my Muenster anyway," mutters Georges, hiding a smile.

"I cannot buy what I cannot taste," says Alexander. "Such a disappointment – I had heard such wondrous rumours. Good thing I didn't buy anything sight unseen!" On his shoulder, the tiny monkey shakes its fist and laughs.

"Who had the combination to the safe besides you and your sister?" asks Velma.

"Nobody," Rosa answers. "I programmed the code for the train's safe myself."

"Let's look at that safe for clues," says Fred.

If Fred examines the inside of the safe, turn to page 42.

If Fred inspects the outside of the safe, turn to page 85.

Scooby leans to the right – and guesses wrong!

The mouse zooms around him with the chunk of cheese, and it disappears through the little hole in the door.

Scooby and the gang push through the door as quickly as they can, but there's no sign of the mouse . . . or the cheese.

"Rare rid rit ro?" Scooby wonders.

"Don't worry, Scooby," Shaggy assures him. "We'll find that mouse!"

"Where should we look?" asks Velma. "In the cattle carriage? Or maybe it went outside by the milk tank carriage!"

If the gang searches for the mouse in the cattle car, turn to page 41.

If they investigate the milk tank car, turn to page 75.

With a screech, Zips jumps off of Alexander's shoulder. He presses the automatic door button and exits the luggage carriage.

"Excuse me," says Alexander. "I must follow my monkey."

"There's no cheese here anyway," says Georges, and he hurries along the aisle, leaving through the other side.

Roberto says, "We will report this to the authorities." He and Rosa stride away, too, following Georges.

Velma huddles up with her friends. "Who do you suspect and why?" she asks. "Georges Fromage may gain the most from the mozzarella being missing."

"Maybe Rosa," says Fred. "She has the code."

"Rosa's hiding something," says Daphne.

"I don't trust Alexander Iskender," Shaggy argues.

If the gang investigates Georges Fromage, turn to page 97.

If they suspect Rosa Robbiolo, turn to page 24.

If they check out Alexander Iskender, turn to page 36.

The gang escort Rosa through the train until they find a portly policeman.

"Excuse me, officer," says Fred. "We have Rosa Robbiolo, who is guilty of stealing her brother's cheese!"

The policeman shakes his head. "No," he replies, "she isn't."

"I could have told you so," says Rosa. "If you'd listened to me."

"How do you know?" Velma asks the officer.

"Because we caught the real culprit," he answers. "It would be illegal for me to tell you who that is . . . but it is not Rosa Robbiolo."

"Like, we're very sorry," says Shaggy.

"Sorry is not enough," says Rosa with a nasty smile. "Officer, I want these kids ejected from the train at the next stop!"

And that's exactly what happens.

The Mystery Inc. gang never finds out who stole the million-dollar mozzarella.

THE END

To follow another path, turn to page 14.

The King of Cheese steps slowly towards the teenagers, his cape swirling behind him. Zips bares his teeth and chitters nastily.

"Like, I don't like the look on Alexander's face," says Shaggy nervously.

"Run!" cries Scooby.

Velma peers around as the gang backs up, away from Alexander atop his fancy lounge carriage. "But which way?" she asks.

If the gang hops carriages and heads down into Alexander's stateroom, turn to page 19.

If they run in the other direction and climb into the guard's van, turn to page 82.

If they hurry around Alexander and scramble down the ladder into the lounge, turn to page 92.

They tiptoe over to the safe in the spooky luggage carriage. As soon as Fred touches the safe, the latch clicks, and the door swings open.

Inside is the missing mozzarella! It glows in Fred's torch beam.

"Like, how did that get here?" asks Shaggy. "Someone must have returned it!"

Suddenly a hand reaches past Fred, grabs the cheese, and yanks it away.

"Hey!" cries Daphne. "Give that back!"

"No," spits Georges. "This cheese is too beautiful for you!"

Everyone stumbles as the train starts up and begins chugging through the tunnel again.

"Rab rit!" growls Scooby.

Velma says, "Grab the cheese from Georges!"

"Forget the cheese," says Fred. "Grab Georges! We caught him returning the mozzarella he obviously stole. Let's take him to the police!"

If the gang lunges for the cheese, turn to page 102.

If they drag Georges to the authorities, turn to page 51.

The gang heads towards the milk tank carriage. They pass through the cattle carriage again, staying quiet to not wake the snoring cows.

The milk carriage is the same shape as an oil drum – a large metal cylinder designed to carry liquids. Metal rungs of a ladder stick out from the side.

"Is anyone mad enough to climb up there?" asks Fred. "Should we look inside the milk tank?"

"It's too dangerous for us to check," says Velma. "We could get badly hurt!"

Scooby's teeth chatter.

"I'm scared, too," says Shaggy. "Let's go back to the cattle carriage and check that out."

"We'll be fine if we hold onto the ladder. We should peek inside the tank!" argues Daphne.

If the gang heads back to the cattle carriage, turn to page 41.

If they peek inside the top of the tank, turn to page 22.

The lamp in the lounge goes out, plunging the compartment into darkness.

"Jinkies!" cries Velma.

The lamp flashes and blinks quickly like a strobe light.

Scooby yanks on the hem of Shaggy's shirt when he sees a small green creature crouched menacingly on a little table. The thing has pointy ears, razor claws, and mad eyes. Scooby babbles fearful noises as he pulls harder on Shaggy's shirt.

"It's okay, Scoobs," says Shaggy, sounding scared himself. "It's just a short in the lamp."

Then Shaggy sees where Scooby is pointing – at the creepy little fiend.

It bares rows of sharp teeth in a mean grin. Shaggy jumps into Scooby's arms in terror.

Great-Aunt Ida stands on her armchair. "Gremlin!" she shrieks. "Run away! Before it bites!"

If the gang runs away, turn to page 100.

If they try to grab the gremlin, turn to page 25.

Daphne peers at the passengers' suitcases on the racks in the luggage carriage. "Let's peek in some of these suitcases," she says.

"That is a bad idea," says Velma.

Fred shines his torch on the latch on the nearest chest. As Daphne fumbles with the lock, suddenly the entire train shudders. A powerful rumble knocks everybody to the floor. The sound of dirt and stones falling on top of the train echoes around them.

"Is it the end of the world?" cries Shaggy.

"No," says Velma, "but this may be worse – I think the tunnel is collapsing!"

"I don't want to be squashed by a mountain!" whimpers Daphne.

Scooby sobs miserably into Shaggy's arms.

The gang huddles around Scooby in a group hug, expecting at any moment for boulders to crash through the ceiling and crush them all.

Turn to page 38.

"I'd rather play cards," says Velma. "I want to choose the deck, though."

"Fair enough," says Rosa.

Velma goes to the rack of games along the wall and picks up a large, fancy wooden box of playing cards. She carries it over to Rosa's table and opens it.

Rosa shrieks as a tiny mouse pops up.

It's carrying a chunk of the million-dollar mozzarella.

"Where did it get that?" asks Daphne.

"No idea," says Fred, "but don't let that mouse get away!"

The mouse jumps from the box, carrying the cheese, and scurries across the floor towards a little hole in the door.

Scooby blocks the mouse. He and the mouse have a standoff.

If Scooby-Doo should lean left to block the mouse, turn to page 67.

If he should lean right, turn to page 69.

The gremlin screeches at the gang when they enter the stateroom. It hops onto Alexander's folded bed, whistling furiously. The window is open behind it.

"Grab it!" shouts Velma.

Shaggy and Scooby rush at the gremlin, but it jumps and they crash into one another.

The gremlin swings on the curtains, swooping over Fred. It lands on Alexander's luggage rack and knocks into a small box. The gremlin and the box tumble to the floor. With another whistle, the gremlin zooms between Daphne's feet, bounces onto the bed, and vanishes out of the window.

"C'mon," cries Velma. "Let's climb out!"

"Did you hear it whistling?" asks Shaggy. "Like, I wonder if we can just whistle for it to come back."

"Wait," says Daphne. "What's in that box?"

If they follow the gremlin out of the window, turn to page 15.

If they try whistling, turn to page 45.

If they investigate the box, turn to page 19.

With his blonde hair flattened, Georges Fromage sits up in the dining carriage. His eyes fill with tears. "Why did you tackle me so hard?" he whines. "That hurt!"

"Why are you scaring these nice people?" asks Daphne.

"Oh, I am so sorry!" sobs Georges. Tears roll down his cheeks. "The costume, it was childish, I know! But I couldn't see what else to do. The kitchen cooks were so rude to me . . . and I had to do something to fight back!"

"Like, that doesn't make any sense," says Shaggy.

"Reah," says Scooby, scratching his head.

"I think he stole the million-dollar mozzarella," says Velma. "Let's take him to the authorities!"

"No," cries Georges. "Take pity on me, and I'll explain everything!"

If the gang lets Georges explain more, turn to page 46.
If they take him to the police, turn to page 51.

"I am as surprised as you are!" says Rosa. "First of all, I know better than to squash delicate mozzarella in a Monopoly box! Or to cut it before it's ready to eat."

"You really had no idea the piece of cheese was in there?" asks Velma.

"Of course not," says Rosa.

"Look at Rosa's eyes," suggests Daphne. "She's genuinely confused by this turn of events."

"It's true," replies Rosa. "I am bewildered. Will you help Roberto and me catch the real cheese thief? The main part of the mozzarella is still missing!"

"We'll find the real culprit," swears Fred.

Turn to page 31.

The gang pushes into the guard's van's dark main compartment. Velma flicks a light switch.

A small, bare table is attached to the wall, with three chairs around it. Tacked up on the wall are train maps and a calendar.

Fred says, "There's nothing here–"

A thump behind them makes the guard's van lurch. Everyone grabs onto the table and chairs as they slow abruptly. Scooby falls onto his butt.

"Jinkies," says Velma. "What happened?"

They hurry to the door. Fred yanks it open.

The guard's van is detached from the train!

As they reach a hill, the guard's van slows more, and the train pulls further away.

From atop the lounge carriage, Alexander appears with Zips on his shoulder. "Farewell!" he calls, waving.

The train disappears into the distance, leaving the gang behind.

THE END

To follow another path, turn to page 14.

Scooby bites into the mozzarella, chomping the gourmet cheese. It tastes so good, he can't help gobbling it all down.

"Oh, Scooby," says Velma, "I wish you hadn't done that."

"We do, too," says a voice from the doorway. Standing between train carriages are two police officers in uniform, with Alexander Iskender, Georges Fromage, and Roberto Robbiolo behind them.

"Arrest those kids!" Chef Robbiolo cries. "Their dog ate my beautiful mozzarella. I'm ruined!"

Scooby giggles sheepishly, but he can't deny his guilt – the police saw him chewing the cheese.

The Mystery Inc. gang gets busted for mozzarella theft. The police escort them from the train at the next stop.

When the case comes to court, an angry judge bans them from entering Europe ever again.

THE END

To follow another path, turn to page 14.

Fred searches around the base of the safe, while Velma peers at the top of the metal box.

"Look at this!" says Fred. He holds up a tiny brass button.

"Just like the ones on the monkey's vest," Shaggy points out.

"Rook! Rissing!" says Scooby. He stares right at Zip's vest, where there's a gap in the row of buttons.

"That button has been missing for months," argues Alexander.

"It matches the others exactly," adds Daphne.

"Wait!" calls Velma. She holds up a short straight hair and blinks at it. "It's blonde."

Georges clutches his blonde spiky hair in both hands. "That means nothing!" he exclaims. "Many people have blonde hair!"

Turn to page 70.

In the games room in the front of the train, instead of Roberto, the gang finds Rosa. She sits on a padded bench in front of a low table, playing patience.

Across the carriage are shelves of board games and a larger table, around which four old women play cards.

The gang watches Rosa play for a moment. She shuffles like an expert and lays down cards with a professional snap.

"Definitely not her first time playing cards," notices Fred.

"Like, let's play something with her," says Shaggy. "I love board games."

"Stay focused," says Velma. "We're investigating a theft. Let's ask her directly about what she was doing when the mozzarella was stolen."

If the gang asks Rosa to play games, turn to page 27.

If they ask her direct questions about her alibi, turn to page 54.

Shaggy whistles ten notes of a happy tune.

The gremlin repeats the whistle perfectly. It climbs into view and perches on the window frame.

"Wait," says Daphne. She yanks the gremlin's pointy ear. A rubber mask slips upwards and off.

It's Zips! The monkey screeches and bolts outside again.

"It looked fake," says Daphne, smiling.

"I think I've got this mystery figured out," says Velma. "Let's find the authorities and report Alexander Iskender – and Zips – for the theft of the million-dollar mozzarella."

"Ruh?" blurts Scooby, confused.

"Just follow along," says Velma. "Where do we contact the authorities, in the guard's van or the luggage carriage?"

If the gang heads to the luggage carriage, turn to page 55.

If they enter the guard's van, turn to page 82.

"All clues point to Alexander stealing the mozzarella," cries Velma, "with the help of that monkey! Grab them!"

The whole gang rushes towards Alexander. Zips screeches and shakes his fist.

When they get close to Alexander, he suddenly swirls his cape like a toreador and sidesteps.

The gang stumbles into the cape, getting tangled up together.

Zips laughs as they tumble headlong off the train.

Turn to page 104.

"Explain quickly," says Daphne, waving Rosa's high heel. "This better be good!"

"Okay," says Rosa. "With Roberto's mozzarella stolen, the cattle and the milk in the tank carriage became so much more precious to us. It is our only way to make more of the million-dollar mozzarella!"

"I won't be able to make the cheese in time for the contest," adds Roberto, "but the cattle and milk are our whole future. We were just protecting what was ours by scaring thieves away!"

"Oh," says Shaggy. "You're protecting your cows. Like, that makes a crazy kind of sense."

"It does," admits Velma.

Turn to page 31.

"I'm bored with this cheese story," says Daphne. "We don't need to get involved in this drama."

"Reah," agrees Scooby.

So the members of Mystery Inc. enjoy their dinner in the dining carriage. Scooby-Doo and Shaggy both love their fish and chips so much that they eat two portions each.

Although they have a lovely time on the train and admire the beautiful scenery, nothing too exciting happens on the way to Paris.

It was a nice trip.

THE END

To follow another path, turn to page 14.

Even Scooby-Doo, who will eat anything, feels grossed out by the Aglöö.

"No, thank you," says Daphne. "It will spoil our dinner."

"Your misfortune," says Alexander. He cuts a slice. The cheese drips with gooey blue mould. "Mmm," he murmurs, chewing it. "Delectable."

Great-Aunt Ida peers up. "Aglöö!" she caws.

Alexander cuts some Aglöö for his aunt, who gobbles down the chunk. Cheese smears her lips.

"Mr Iskender," says Fred, "did you have access to the luggage carriage?"

"For my own merchandise," Alexander holds his stomach. His face turns green. "But how could I know Chef Robbiolo's safe code? Excuse me," he gulps. "I need the facilities." Alexander rushes out into the guard's van with Zips.

"That cheese didn't agree with him," says Velma.

They glance at Ida, who sips her tea contentedly.

Turn to page 76.

The gang rushes to the right, trying to go around Alexander to get to the ladder into the lounge.

Scooby-Doo is in the lead. He isn't running fast enough, and Shaggy bumps him accidentally from behind. Scooby loses his balance, and his paws lose their grip on the metal roof. "Ruh-roh," he gasps. Then he slips and falls flat with his legs spread in four directions.

Velma, Fred, and Daphne trip over Scooby's legs. Shaggy topples onto Scooby and grabs him around the waist. They both tumble in a ball, snarling Daphne, Velma, and Fred, too. In a big tangled pile, the whole gang rolls out of control across the roof.

Alexander and Zips howl in laughter as the members of Mystery Inc. whoosh over the edge . . . and plummet off the speeding train.

Turn to page 104.

"Everyone okay?" calls Fred in the inky blackness of the observation carriage.

"I'm unhurt," says Velma.

"Like, A-okay here," says Shaggy. "Just bruised."

"Ree, roo," agrees Scooby with a giggle.

"I'm fine," says Daphne, "but Georges isn't saying anything!"

"Georges?" asks Fred. "Are you all right?"

Two strips of yellow safety lights flicker on along the centre aisle. The gang sees other passengers helping their friends and family up from the floor. Nobody looks injured.

"Georges is gone!" cries Daphne. Next to her is an empty spot where Chef Fromage sat moments before.

"That's very suspicious," says Velma. "We should look for him."

"But where?" asks Fred.

If the gang searches for Georges towards the luggage carriage, turn to page 16.

If they head towards the kitchen carriage, turn to page 50.

The gang keeps battling Chef Fromage for possession of the mozzarella. The cheese stretches surprisingly long as they struggle.

Scooby trips! He grabs onto the handle of the emergency exit door, which pops open. Wind rushes into the observation carriage. A loop of the stretched mozzarella wiggles outside the train and snags on a tall pole.

The entire gang – and Georges – get pulled towards the open emergency exit by the taut mozzarella.

They all scream.

If the gang yanks the cheese even harder, turn to page 32.
If Scooby bites through the stretching cheese, turn to page 84.

"Okay," says Velma. "I'm scared. Run!"

The gang runs down the aisle of the cattle carriage, racing towards the end, away from the ghost cow.

When they reach the door, Fred yanks it open . . . but there's nowhere to go! The milk carriage is connected to the cattle carriage, and there's no walkway.

In the rear of the pack, Scooby, terrified out of his mind by the ghost cow behind him, keeps running blindly. He crashes into the gang, and they all tumble out of the door.

They smash into the curved end of the milk tank and bounce to the side. Then they fall into empty air, off the train.

Turn to page 35.

The Mystery Inc. gang heads in the direction Georges Fromage departed.

They peer around the observation carriage. The entire ceiling is curved glass, offering amazing views of the landscape outside. The train passes through misty foothills, with the shadow of breathtaking mountains up ahead.

"Oh, isn't it pretty?" sighs Daphne. She sits on a cushioned bench in an empty spot among other travellers. "Let's enjoy the view."

Shaggy and Scooby plop down beside her. On Scooby's other side, a skinny man wearing a beret holds binoculars to his eyes.

"Like, I don't see that Fromage person anyhow," says Shaggy.

"Let's keep looking," urges Velma. "Georges is my number one suspect."

The skinny man lowers his binoculars. "Am I now?" he asks.

"Sorry, Chef Fromage," says Fred, "but could we ask you a few questions?"

Turn to page 39.

Fred pushes a table in front of the screeching gremlin, blocking it. Then he quickly helps up Daphne, and bolts after Velma, Shaggy, and Scooby, who are already running for the lounge's exit.

When the gang enters the section between the lounge carriage and Alexander's private stateroom, the train suddenly swings around a sharp turn. Scooby-Doo tumbles against Shaggy, and the two of them fall into the rubber accordion that encloses the space between carriages.

The whole section of rubber tears loose, and the wind pulls it free from the train like a giant kite. The gang tumbles off the train inside the rubber accordion – flying into the air above a grassy embankment.

They all scream in terror as they sail over a marshy field on the gliding rubber cover.

Turn to page 104.

"Like, all Georges wants is his cheese on pizza," says Shaggy. "He didn't steal the mozzarella."

"Yes!" cries Georges. He hugs Scooby around the neck. "Finally I am understood!"

Daphne smiles. "I have an idea," she says. She leads Georges and the gang into the kitchen carriage and knocks on the door.

"Yes?" the cook asks.

"I would love a pizza made with Muenster cheese," Daphne says. "Could you make that for me, please?"

The cook doesn't look happy, but he agrees. Half an hour later, Georges and the gang enjoy Muenster pizza in the dining carriage. It's delicious.

Georges couldn't be happier. "You are the best Americans I've ever met!" he tells the gang when they say good-bye to him.

Turn to page 65.

In the flashing light, the gremlin looks terrifying. Everyone panics, throwing the lounge into chaos.

Scooby, still carrying Shaggy, scurries to the other side of the carriage. He trips over Daphne's feet and tumbles into Velma. They all collapse in a heap at the base of Great-Aunt Ida's armchair.

The gremlin leaps off the table, swings around the flashing lamp, and launches at Fred's head.

Fred ducks. He rolls out of the way and springs back up into a crouch.

With a scary giggle, the gremlin creeps closer to Fred, extending its claws.

Ida bounces on the armchair cushion. "Get it!" she screams. "Watch out! The gremlin's bite is poisonous!"

If Fred tries to grab the gremlin, turn to page 25.
If he backs away slowly, turn to page 60.

The gang searches the entire length of the train, passing through the luggage carriage and a cattle carriage holding cows in pens, until they reach a tank carriage filled with milk. There's no way to walk past the tank carriage – there's a ladder to climb onto its roof.

They find no sign of Roberto anywhere, so they regroup in the luggage carriage.

"That's strange," says Daphne. "He vanished."

"Maybe he slipped past us," suggests Velma.

"He could be in the games room," says Fred. "Maybe we should search there."

"Like, Roberto could've hidden in the cattle pens," guesses Shaggy. "Let's check the cow carriage again."

"Rilk, roo," says Scooby.

"Yeah, Scoobs," replies Shaggy, "there's something funny about the milk carriage, too. We could investigate that more closely."

If the gang searches for Roberto on the milk tanker carriage, turn to page 75.

If they look at the cattle carriage, turn to page 41.

If they walk up to the games room, turn to page 86.

Georges flees the luggage carriage, carrying the mozzarella. Scooby and Shaggy catch up with him in the observation carriage just as the train pulls out of the tunnel, revealing a mountainous landscape all around.

"Rhat's not rours!" cries Scooby. He grabs the top of the mozzarella, but Georges has a good grip on the bottom.

"It's not yours, either!" shouts Georges. "You let go!"

As Georges pulls back, the rest of the gang surrounds Scooby and helps him pull. But Georges is surprisingly strong and doesn't give up.

The mozzarella starts to stretch.

The cheese gets longer and longer as Georges and the gang struggle in their tug of war.

If they keep trying to wrestle the mozzarella from Fromage, turn to page 95.

If Scooby bites through the stretchy cheese, turn to page 84.

The gang falls towards the ground, screaming.

Instead of hitting hard dirt, they splash into cold, muddy water.

They land, unhurt, in a murky pond. All around them are tall bulrushes, buzzing dragonflies, and frogs on lily pads. The mud in the shallow pond squelches under them.

"There goes the train," says Velma glumly. She looks up to watch the train continue on its track, leaving them behind in the muddy pond, until it disappears completely into the distance.

"Ugh," says Daphne, wiping muck from her hair. "This is so gross."

A frog jumps onto Scooby-Doo's head. It croaks.

Scooby peers up at the frog and giggles nervously . . . before he slumps his shoulders and lets out a sad sigh.

THE END

To follow another path, turn to page 14.

"It's just a guy in a rat costume!" cries Velma. "He's not allowed to frighten innocent people. Grab him!"

Fred rushes at the giant rat. At first the rat tries to scare Fred by screeching and holding up its claws, but when Fred doesn't stop running, the rat looks alarmed. It squeals and flees in the opposite direction.

With a leap, Fred grabs the rat around its furry legs, tackling it to the ground.

The rat flops forward, hitting the floor hard. The head of its costume pops off and rolls nearby.

Velma peers down at the blonde hair of the man in the costume. "No surprise," she says with a smile.

Turn to page 80.

AUTHOR

J. E. Bright is the author of many novels, novelizations, and novelty books for children and young adults. He lives in a sunny flat in the Washington Heights neighbourhood of Manhattan, New York City, with his difficult but soft cat, Mabel, and his sweet kitten, Bernard.

ILLUSTRATOR

Scott Neely has been a professional illustrator and designer for many years. For the last eight years, he's been an official Scooby-Doo and Cartoon Network artist, working on such licenced properties as Dexter's Laboratory, Johnny Bravo, Courage the Cowardly Dog, Powerpuff Girls, and more. He has also worked on Pokémon, Mickey Mouse Clubhouse, My Friends Tigger & Pooh, Handy Manny, Strawberry Shortcake, Bratz, and many other popular characters. He lives in a suburb of Philadelphia and has a scrappy Yorkshire Terrier, Alfie.

GLOSSARY

abashed (uh-BASHT) – made to feel embarrassed

alibi (AL-uh-bye) – a claim that a person accused of a crime was somewhere else when the crime occurred

coax (KOHKS) – to persuade someone to do something, gradually or by flattery

compartment (kuhm-PAHRT-muhnt) – a separate part of a container or vehicle

convention (kuhn-VEN-shuhn) – a formal gathering of people who share a common profession or interest

culprit (KUHL-prit) – a person who is guilty

customary (KUS-tuh-m-ee) – happening by habit

decline (di-KLINE) – to refuse something politely

hunch (HUHNCH) – an idea that is based on a feeling you have and is not based on facts or information

illuminated (i-LOO-muh-nate-id) – brought to light

maître d' (may-truh-DI) – the head waiter

meddle (MED-uhl) – to get involved in someone else's personal business

toreador (TOR-ee-uh-dor) – a bullfighter

trestle (TRES-uhl) – a frame shaped like the letter A that supports a bridge or railway track

YOU CHOOSE JOKES!

YOU CHOOSE which punch line is funniest!

What do you say if Scooby-Doo wants your cheese?
a. "Get away! It's nacho cheese!"
b. "This cheese is too Gouda for you!"
c. "I already feta piece to you!"

What do you get if you cross a hunk of cheese with Frankenstein?
a. A scary Muenster.
b. A huge explosion and then nothing but de brie.
c. I don't know, but you better Edam up before he eats you!

What does Scooby like on a pizza?
a. Extra cheese.
b. Extra everything.
c. His teeth!

What did the boy cheese say to the girl cheese?

a. I'm very fondue!

b. I Camembert it when you're gone!

c. I become blue without you!

What is an orca's favourite cheese?

a. Limb-burger.

b. Edam.

c. Shark cheddar

What did the cheese say to the grater?

a. "Ha ha, you really cut me up!"

b. "I was very offended by what you shred about me!"

c. "You always rub me the wrong way!"

SCOOBY-DOO!

THE CHOICE IS YOURS!

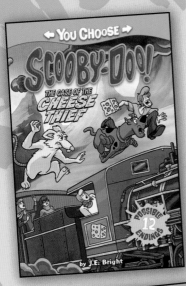

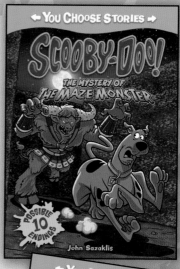